CHILDREN
ICR
S
    Stevens, Philippa J.
    Bonk! goes the ball /
    LAT 1034754554

NOV 1 9 1999

D0579111

A ROOKIE READER®

BONK!
GOES THE BALL

By Philippa J. Stevens

Illustrations by Clovis Martin

Prepared under the direction of Robert Hillerich, Ph.D.

CHILDRENS PRESS®

CHICAGO

LIBRARY OF CONGRESS
Library of Congress Cataloging-in-Publication Data

Stevens, Philippa J.
    Bonk! goes the ball / by Philippa J. Stevens ;
illustrations by Clovis Martin ; prepared under the
direction of Robert Hillerich.
        p.   cm. — (A Rookie reader)
    Summary: A ball is hit, kicked, chased, passed, and
sent through a goal during a soccer game.
    ISBN 0-516-02061-7
    [1. Balls (Sporting goods)—Fiction.
2. Soccer—Fiction.] I. Martin, Clovis, ill. II. Hillerich,
Robert L., 1927-   . III. Title. IV. Series.
PZ7.S84545Bo   1990
[E]—dc20   89-48561
                                                            CIP
                                                            AC

Copyright © 1990 by Childrens Press®, Inc.
All rights reserved. Published simultaneously in Canada.
Printed in the United States of America.
        9 10 R 99 98

Here comes the ball!

Woops!
Missed the ball.

Where is the ball?

Kick the ball.

Oops!
Don't catch the ball.

Follow the ball,

chase the ball,

pass the ball, and

steal the ball.

Woops!
There goes the ball!

Hit the ball
with my head

14

or with my knee.
Bonk!

Find the ball.

18

Kick the ball.
Missed the ball
and landed on my back!

Stop the ball.
Now I've got the ball.
Move the ball to the spot.

Look at the ball.
Watch the ball and
step back.

Watch the ball
and step back.

Watch the ball.
Run and kick!

Goal!

WORD LIST

and	goal	look	steal
at	goes	missed	step
back	got	move	stop
ball	head	my	the
bonk	here	now	there
catch	hit	on	to
chase	is	oops	watch
comes	I've	or	where
don't	kick	pass	with
find	knee	run	woops
follow	landed	spot	

About the Author

Philippa Stevens is a native of a small market town of Petersfield, Hampshire, England. From 1982 to 1989 she lived in the United States and taught pre-school and kindergarten children at the Children's House Montessori School.

Her goals for the next few years include writing more children's stories, finishing her degree with the Open University, and introducing her son to the historical sites and scenic beauty of England.

Other than writing, Philippa Stevens enjoys reading, jazz and classical music, and sports. While in the United States, she helped coach her son's soccer and baseball teams.

About the Artist

Clovis Martin is a graduate of the Cleveland Institute of Art. During a varied career he has art directed, designed and illustrated a variety of reading, educational, and other products for children. He resides with his wife and daughter in Cleveland Heights, Ohio.

1034754554